Stone Me

When a new supply teacher called Ms Dusa turns up at the
school wearing a large turban over her hair, Perce and
Andy get suspicious. After several children in the class get
turned into stone the duo realise that they are right, this is
indeed Medusa come into the twenty-first century.
As none of the grown-ups seem to rumble as to what is
happening, Perce and Andy decide that action needs to be
taken and they are the ones to take it.

A hilarious take on the ancient Greek myth.

Other books by Steve Barlow & Steve Skidmore

Steve Barlow & Steve Skidmore

STONE ME!

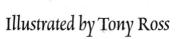

Illustrated by Tony Ross

BARN OWL BOOKS

Stone Me! was first published by Dutton in 1995
This edition first published 2005 by Barn Owl Books
157 Fortis Green Road, London N10 3LX
Barn Owl Books are distributed by Frances Lincoln,
4 Torriano Mews, Torriano Avenue, London NW5 2RZ

ISBN 1-903015-43-X

Text copyright © 1995, 2005 Steve Barlow & Steve Skidmore
Illustrations copyright © 1995, 2005 Tony Ross

Designed and typeset by Douglas Martin Associates
Printed and bound in China by Imago

Contents

Chapter One

THE CAR FROM
ANOTHER PLANET

"School should be banned," Perce snarled. "It's a Cruel and Unusual Punishment."

Perce and Andy were trudging towards their school down streets still damp from the previous night's rain. Andy was rhythmically kicking a football from foot to foot. This was getting on Perce's nerves. She would have been more impressed if the ball hadn't been in a plastic carrier bag, or if Andy had at least let go of the handles.

"I mean," Perce went on, "we drag along there day after day and everything's the same, nothing ever happens. It's like the Chinese Water Torture."

The bag handles broke and Andy, scooting after the ball, narrowly avoided being mown down by a milk-float. Perce raised her eyes to heaven.

"What's the Chinese Water Torture?" Andy

wanted to know after they had outdistanced the furious milkman.

"You get tied to a chair and they drip water on your head until you go stark raving mad."

Andy thought about this. "Doesn't sound like much of a torture to me. I mean, if I was James Bond and I got nabbed by some evil genius who wants to rule the world . . ."

Perce gritted her teeth. "Andy . . ."

". . . and I was expecting them to cut me in half with a laser beam . . ."

"Look . . ."

". . . or pull my fingernails out . . ."

"Listen . . ."

". . . and all they did was tie me to a chair and drip water on my head, I reckon I'd probably be quite pleased."

Perce grabbed a handful of Andy's jacket and glared. "What I'm trying to say, brain-sprain, is that every day at school it's the same: boring Maths, boring English, boring Science, I just wish something would HAPPEN!"

Andy pulled away and tapped her on the shoulder. "You're on!"

"What?"

"Off ground tick! We never finished the game last night. You're on!"

Andy started trying to climb on top of a pillar box. Perce, fuming, was about to drag him down when Andy stopped dead with one foot in the letter slot and gaped.

Perce turned to see what he was staring at. She felt her own jaw drop.

"Wow!" breathed Andy, "Look at that!"

With a swish of tyres, a car swung round the corner. In the dingy side street, it looked as out of place as a dragon in a budgie's cage.

"What on Earth IS it?" asked Perce in hushed tones.

"It's nothing on Earth, it's a Car from Another Planet."

Perce shook her head. There were times when she thought Andy must be from Another planet. Still, she had to admit the Car was something out of this world. "Is that its bonnet?"

"It's got to be," Andy muttered. "It's at the front."

They both gazed in awe as the bonnet sailed past. On either side of it, chromed exhaust pipes sprouted. Enormous wings flared out over wheels with glittering silver hubs and white-walled tyres.

"Very tasty," observed Andy, wobbling dangerously on the pillar box.

The main body of the Car followed; two-tone paint, blood-red and midnight black, with a fabric hood above narrow, secret-looking windows.

Finally came the boot, about a mile long, with another huge wheel strapped to its lid.

The engine rumbled like a caged lion. This was clearly a Car that was heading from HERE to

THERE and anybody stupid enough to get in its way was going to end up seriously squished.

"Big, innit?" said Andy, jumping down as the Car swung left at the traffic lights. "Not a local registration number." Andy knew about things like that. "I wonder where it's going?"

"It turned towards the school," said Perce.

Andy gave her a look. "Our school?" he asked in a tone of complete disbelief.

"I only said 'towards'." Being on the defensive annoyed Perce. She thumped Andy on the arm, hard.

"What's that for?"

"Now you're on!" Perce stuck her tongue out at Andy and raced off down the street. Andy, trying not to drop his schoolbag and football, followed.

The school (as Perce put it) had been built when dinosaurs ruled the earth. It was a grim building in red brick with no playing field, and the staff had to park their cars in the yard. Normally, five minutes before the bell, this would be seething with screaming hordes of kids chasing tennis balls, stray dogs and each other. Fuming teachers would be hesitantly guiding their cars through the chaos, pipping their horns in annoyance while their engines overheated.

This morning, though, as Perce and Andy strolled towards the gates, they realised that the playground on the other side of the wall was unnaturally silent.

Andy began to panic. "Oh no! They've gone in, we're late, that's twice this week, Millsey'll do me . . ." He calmed down as Perce pulled up her sleeve and showed him her watch. 8.55. As Andy looked at it, Perce cuffed him with her free hand for yelling at her.

"Ow," moaned Andy. He jerked a thumb at the wall. "Well, if we're not late, what's going on in there?"

"Something's up." Perce began to run. Once again, Andy followed.

As they screeched to a halt in the gateway, Perce saw immediately that every kid in the yard was gazing as if hypnotized towards the end where the staff cars were parked. She and Andy followed their gaze. Standing there, like a racehorse in a line of seaside donkeys, was the Car.

"Stone me," breathed Andy, "it *was* coming here." He gazed at Perce in wonder. "How did you know?" Perce kept her gaze on the Car.

The door opened with an expensive 'chlunk'. The driver got out.

She was very tall and thin. She wore a turban; not the plain, simple sort that the Sikh dads wore when they came to collect their kids, but a purple, shimmering turban, with complicated folds, pinned at the front with a jewelled clasp.

Below the turban, she wore glasses so black you couldn't imagine that they had eyes behind them.

Andy let out his breath in a low whistle. "Spoooky!"

The driver's gloved hands gripped the hem of a full-length velvet cloak, like Dracula's except that it was a sort of glowing green. She set off across the playground towards the school building. Kids stood aside to let her pass. She seemed not to notice the impression she was making; or perhaps she did notice and didn't care.

"Is it a fancy dress party today?" asked Andy.

He said it very quietly, but the woman seemed to hear. As she drew level with Perce and Andy,

she stopped suddenly and turned the dark gaze
of her sunglasses towards them. She raised one
gloved hand to the frame of her glasses. Perce
noticed with astonishment that she wore rings
over the gloves.

Perce stared into the blankness of the woman's
glasses, and suddenly felt very cold. A shiver
passed up her back, through her neck and into the
ends of her hair. She had a sudden strange feeling

that she should know who this woman was – as if the stranger belonged to a past that she had almost completely forgotten.

The woman began to slide the dark glasses forward on her nose. At any moment, her hidden eyes would be revealed. For some reason she couldn't begin to understand, Perce found herself rooted to the spot, incapable of movement, as the glasses slid further and further...

The clatter of the school's electric bells cut through the still air. It was nine o'clock.

The woman instantly pushed her glasses back to the bridge of her nose, dropped her upraised hand and turned away. Perce caught a brief scent of some strange, exotic, heavy perfume as she passed. The woman mounted the steps to the school's main entrance with an efficient tap of heels, and vanished into the building.

The kids began to stir. Mouths snapped shut as their owners realised how stupid they looked. Bags were picked up and kids began to move sheepishly towards their classrooms.

Andy was still gazing awe-struck at the great Car. He rubbed his eyes and blinked. "Wow, some car!"

Mr Latimer, the ageing deputy head, came shambling down the steps to get his briefcase, which he always forgot.

"Sir," Andy called across as he fumbled for his keys, "whose Car's that?"

"The new supply teacher's. And don't stand there like a prune, you'll miss registration." Mr Latimer slammed his car door shut, then opened it again to turn his lights off (he always forgot that, too) before huffing back inside the school.

Andy stared at Perce. "The new supply teacher's?" He eyed the car with amazement. "Have teachers had a pay rise, or what?"

Chapter Two

YEAR ONE MUTANT ZOMBIE WEIRDOES

"Where's Millsey?" Perce asked Syreeta.

Miss Mills was Perce and Andy's class teacher. It was unheard of for her to miss registration.

"Isn't her car here?" asked Andy.

Syreeta sniffed. "Couldn't miss it, if it was." Syreeta was always neat and tidy, and hated mess of any kind. She thoroughly disapproved of Miss Mills' old banger, which was mostly dirt held together by rust.

"I bet she's off sick," said Andy. "We'll have a supply teacher in. Hey, what if it's her with the Car?"

Perce shrugged. She pretended not to be interested when the rest of the class jabbered on about what might have happened to Millsey, and the new teacher's spectacular arrival. You couldn't let on that you were bothered about what teachers did. It might make them think they were important.

She had to admit to herself, though, that the thought of the woman from the Car turning up to teach her class gave Perce the shivers.

"Look out," hissed Eddie Johnson, scampering back to his seat from the doorway, "it's not her from the Car, it's Latimer."

Perce felt strangely disappointed. It wasn't that she disliked old Latimer. At least he could always be sidetracked by questions about anything to do with Ancient Greece. Every summer, he spent his holidays pottering around old temples and places, and insisted on showing his slides at school assemblies. Perce sometimes thought that Latimer looked on Ancient Greece as his job, and school teaching as his hobby. Still, he knew lots of Greek legends, some of which were pretty exciting. Listening to him rambling on about the Trojan Wars was more fun than Maths, and you weren't expected to remember any of it.

"What are you face-aching about?" whispered Andy.

Perce ignored him, and went on scowling. She liked to know everything straight away, and now another class would get the new teacher first. She wondered why. She wouldn't have to ask, of course. Eddie Johnson would do that.

He did. His hand was in the air the instant Mr Latimer stepped through the door. "Why have we got you, sir?"

Mr Latimer raised an eyebrow. "How nice of you to make me feel so welcome."

"Yes, sir, but why?"

"Haven't you got any work to do?" snapped Mr Latimer.

"Lots, sir. Why?"

Mr Latimer sighed. Eddie was famous for his curiosity, and for never giving up on a question until he got an answer. "I'm afraid," he said heavily, "that it looks unlikely that Miss Mills will be returning in the forseeable future."

A buzz rose from the class.

Eddie's hand shot up. "Mr Latimer . . ."

"Before you ask, Edward, I don't know what is the matter with Miss Mills and I wouldn't tell you if I did. The Head has decided that you should

have a permanent class teacher for the rest of your final year. Me, for my sins."

"Who's taking *your* class then, sir?" chimed in Perce.

Mr Latimer shuddered. "Well, Priscilla . . ." Perce squirmed. She HATED being called Priscilla, even if it WAS her name. "I understand," Mr Latimer continued in the tone of voice he used for announcing that some *antisocial hooligan* had been writing graffiti in the boys' toilets *again*, "that the-ah-new supply teacher will take over my class." Mr Latimer coughed disapprovingly. And with that he began to take the register.

The minute the bell went for break, Perce and Andy made straight for the kids from Mr Latimer's old class. Perce was determined to find out as much as she could about the new teacher.

The first years were known to the older kids as "stickies". This was because constant runny noses and dribbles of sweets, soft drinks and ice-cream made them as disgustingly tacky as a newly painted wall. The stickies never normally got any sort of attention from the older kids, apart from the occasional shove if they got in the way. However, that first break after the new teacher's arrival, they were surrounded. It seemed that Perce and Andy weren't the only ones who wanted to know all about the mystery woman from the Car. The trouble was, the younger kids weren't saying much.

Perce beckoned a couple of stickies over. They looked at her. They looked at each other. Knowing what was good for them, they edged warily across the yard to where Perce and Andy waited. Perce started the interrogation.

"You've had the new teacher this morning, right?" The stickies looked at each other and nodded dumbly. "What's she like?"

The stickies looked at each other again. "Like?

Perce clenched her fists, but you could have spread her voice on toast.

"Yes." She smiled sweetly. "What sort of a person is she?"

The younger kids looked at the ground for a change. They shuffled their feet.

"She's all right," one muttered.

I'm going to kill them, thought Perce. Both of them. One after the other.

Andy had a go. "She looks a bit scary. Is she?"
More shuffling.

"Well . . . she's a bit strict . . ." Sticky Number One began hesitantly.

". . . yeah – but she's all right," Sticky Number Two added hurriedly.

"Oh, yeah, she's all right."

Perce felt as if she was trying to run in soft sand. Her patience was wearing very thin, but she went on.

Did the new teacher shout? Not really. Was she

strange? How did Perce mean strange? Well, was she funny? She didn't tell jokes. Not funny ha ha, was she mad? She was just all right.

All over the yard, other people were trying to drag information out of the new teacher's class, but nobody was getting any further. Well'ard Wally, the school hard nut (so called because he reckoned he was well-hard, but in fact was a bit of a wally) tried his usual strong-arm tactics, but even he could get nothing more out of the stickies. The only thing they seemed sure of was the new teacher's name, and that was as weird as anything else about her. Apparently it was "Dusa". Mrs or Miss? Perce wanted to know. "Ms," was the reply.

Before the end of break, Perce and Andy had given up in disgust.

Lunch was served in the assembly hall, which was now full of the din of cutlery clashing against plates, Well'ard Wally cheeking harassed lunch supervisors, and the usual complaints about the food. As they waited for lunch with Lee Adams and Eddie Johnson, Perce and Andy tried to make sense of the stickies' strange behaviour.

"Are they all thick?" asked Andy.

Perce thought about this. "Well, they are only first years," she said, "but there's more to it than that."

"They just look straight through you," said Lee, examining his salad for caterpillars.

"Like zombies," Eddie chimed in. "Mutant Zombie Weirdoes." He dragged his sweatshirt over his head like a hood and pulled faces. The others ignored him.

"D'you reckon they're scared?" suggested Andy.

Perce took a yoghurt. "Not really. They'd look more miserable. You know what it's like when you've done something and you don't want anybody to find out . . ."

When you didn't want a teacher to know what was going on, thought Perce, you kept out of the way, tried to change the subject, avoided the teacher's eye. But this was different.

"It's not that they don't want to say anything," she said, "they just haven't got anything to say."

Eddie considered this. "You mean like they can't remember what happened in class?"

"Yes." The queue moved forward.

"But that's daft," protested Andy, "we saw her class at break, she'd only just finished teaching them, they must have remembered."

"You'd think so, wouldn't you?"

They found a table and put their trays down. Perce waved a chip under Andy's nose.

"Why are they playing dumb?"

Andy, Lee and Eddie looked at each other and shrugged.

Eddie pointed at Lee's chips. "I'll have some of them."

"You wish."

"That's too many chips for somebody who's on a diet."

Lee glared at him. "I'm not on a diet."

"Well, you should be. Obesity caused by fatty foods and lack of exercise is a major health risk. It was on the news."

Lee glared at Eddie. "Who are you calling obese . . . ?"

As Lee and Eddie bickered, Andy pointed to Perce's sausage roll. "I'll have that if you don't want it."

Perce looked at it in horror. "Did I pick that out? Why didn't you tell me? You know I don't like sausage rolls."

Andy speared it on his fork and grinned at her. "But I do."

By the end of the week, Perce was ready to foam at the mouth. There was something very disturbing about Ms Dusa and Perce, who prided herself on knowing what teachers were up to and what made them tick, was nowhere near even guessing what it was.

"What's wrong with Ms Dusa?" Perce asked Andy as they wandered home.

Andy shrugged. "She's just weird."

Perce snorted. "All teachers are weird."

Andy nodded: "Yeah, but she's turbo-charged mega-weird – even for a teacher. I mean, just think about her clothes. They're REALLY weird; all those cloaks and capes."

"And gloves," agreed Perce. "She never takes them off."

"And those turbans. Have you seen her without a turban?" Andy added.

"And has anyone seen her take her sunglasses off, even when it's really cloudy?" Perce felt that they were on to something.

"Maybe she's got something wrong with her eyes," Andy suggested.

"Ha!" Perce gave Andy a look of deep scorn. "And what about assemblies?"

Andy shuddered. "I know what you mean."

The morning assembly at Perce and Andy's school was usually pretty dull. The Head would

give one of her little talks about Courtesy Costs
Nothing, or Latimer would ramble on about an
interesting bit of a Greek urn he'd found (Eddie
would crack the same old joke about "What's a
Greek urn? – Ten euros a week!"). There would be

muffled sniggers and whispers as everyone caught
up with everyone else's news, and the teachers did-
n't make a fuss as long as the noise didn't get out
of hand. But since Ms Dusa's arrival, anyone who
even thought about whispering would feel a
prickling on the back of the neck, and turn to meet
the supply teacher's dark gaze. Assemblies had
suddenly got very quiet.

"And she never shouts," Perce continued.

"That's not natural – all teachers shout. Yesterday, I hung around in the corridor outside her class-room and all I could hear was Ms Dusa telling her kids what to do in a really quiet voice. And there wasn't any noise coming out of the class."

"Well, some classes are quiet. We are for Latimer," countered Andy.

"Not THAT quiet. And what about her name?"

"What about it?"

"I looked it up in the telephone directory." They had reached the gate of Andy's house but Perce pulled him back. "There isn't a 'Dusa' in the whole of the book."

Andy considered this for a moment, and bright-ened. "Maybe she's a spy – or maybe I was right about the Car being from another planet. Yeah, that's it – she's an alien!"

Perce pushed Andy through his gate and went home. Aliens! Hah! She liked Andy but there were times when he was as daft as a brush.

"Mum, d'you reckon there really are such things as aliens?"

"What?"

"Andy thinks we're being taught by aliens."

"Sssssh." Perce's mum was trying to listen to The Archers.

"If all the kids at that school are like you," her father remarked, "I don't reckon it's the *teachers* who are the aliens."

"It's not funny, Dad. This new one, Ms Dusa, she's really weird."

"Hark who's talking."

Perce remembered how the new teacher had stopped and stared at her in the yard, and shivered. "I don't think she likes me."

"I can't say I blame her."

"Thanks, Dad."

"Only joking. Have you seen my pullover?"

"You're sitting on it!"

Perce sighed. Parents! You talk to them, they talk to you; it would be handy if you spoke the same language. Anyway, what could she tell them? That Ms Dusa's class was quiet? But ALL classes were supposed to be quiet, weren't they? And she wears dark glasses. Poor woman, probably something wrong with her eyes. And she stared at me and I got this creepy feeling I've known her before but I don't know where or when . . . Now, Perce, you're letting your imagination run away with you again . . .

Too true, thought Perce, my imagination's working itself up to smash the world record for the hundred metres panic-stricken sprint.

"One thing's for sure," she told Andy when he came around a few minutes later to see if Perce fancied a kick-around in the park. "My parents aren't going to believe that a teacher is seriously weird just because I say so. I'm on my own."

"Well – I'm with you."

Perce gave Andy a look. "Exactly. I'm on my own."

"Thanks."

Perce spent the next few days in a state of puzzled apprehension.

Everybody at school seemed to be talking about Ms Dusa except the kids in her class. The stickies should have been more interested than anyone else in finding out about their new teacher, but they didn't seem interested at all. And the blankness they had shown when asked questions about her that first break had, if anything, got even blanker.

But Perce had another reason to feel worried. Several times during assembly, or at breaktimes, she felt a sudden chill and turned to find Ms Dusa's dark sunglasses apparently fixed on her, even when she had done nothing to attract attention. This made Perce very uncomfortable; she couldn't help thinking there was something she should know or remember about the new teacher, but what? Why should Ms Dusa seem interested in her?

As the days went by and nothing more happened, Perce began to tell herself she'd been stupid. Ms Dusa was a perfectly normal teacher, if there was such a thing. If Ms Dusa liked big cars and strange clothes, good luck to her; about time we had a bit of colour round here. She wasn't really interested in Perce. Her kids were quiet because they were dopey first-year stickies. Everything's OK, Perce told herself.

That was before the terrible thing that happened to Eddie Johnson.

Chapter Three

THE TERRIBLE THING THAT HAPPENED TO EDDIE JOHNSON

The strange, odd and altogether peculiar thing about Eddie Johnson was that he actually liked school. Nearly everybody liked *some* things about school. Even Perce had been heard to admit that the breaks were OK, and Andy reckoned the football games in the yard were often pretty good. But Eddie even liked the *lessons* – Eddie loved school and never, *ever* missed it.

Perce and Andy had always thought that this wasn't normal. Most kids they knew went to sleep hoping that there would be something wrong with them when they woke up (preferably something involving spots but no pain) so they could stay at home in bed, play computer games and watch videos. But not Eddie. Even when he'd

broken his leg after an unfortu-
nate incident involving Andy,
Perce and a fire extinguisher,
he'd insisted on coming in to
school a few days later with
his leg in plaster, hopping
around on crutches like Long
John Silver.

He also fancied himself as a detective. Anytime
anybody lost something,
Eddie would launch into
detailed investigations, inter-
view witnesses, search for
clues and generally make
such a fuss that whoever had
lost the thing Eddie was
looking for would feel sorry

they'd ever mentioned it, even if it turned up,
which it hardly ever did. Eddie never let up.

That was why when he
started to take an interest
in Ms Dusa, Perce started
to feel very uneasy
indeed. The more she

34

thought about Ms Dusa and her class's strange behaviour, the more Perce felt that there were things about Ms Dusa she would much rather not know.

So Perce wasn't exactly delighted when, as she was standing in the playground watching an argument between two boys gradually turn into a fight, Eddie Johnson came sneaking round the corner with his collar up round his ears and said, "Pssssst!"

Perce decided to ignore him.

"Pssssssssssssssst!"

Perce ignored Eddie again, but much harder this time.

Andy strolled over. "What's up?"

"It's Eddie," Perce told him. "He's sprung a leak."

"No, listen." Eddie pawed at Perce's sleeve. "I've got an idea."

"Phone the *Guinness Book of Records*."

"Look, you know Dusa's car?" Eddie beckoned Perce to draw nearer.

Perce wondered whether just to walk away, but Mr Latimer had appeared and broken up what had promised to be quite an interesting fight, much to her disgust. And although she was convinced that Eddie was several crisps short of a packet, there was something about his excitement that made both Perce and Andy move in closer to hear what the great thought was. Eddie looked around to check that no one was near, drew in his breath and announced . . .

"Ms Dusa's car – is *strange!*"

Perce looked at Andy. Andy looked at Perce. They both looked at Eddie.

"Really? That's the big news, is it? Ms Dusa's car is *strange?*" Perce snorted. "Yes, considering it looks like no other car on the road, is far too flash for a teacher to own and according to Andy comes from outer space, I suppose you could call it strange."

"Ah," said Eddie, beaming, "but I know *why* it's strange, and you don't."

I'm going to hate myself for asking this, thought Perce. "Well, why?"

"You know Latimer?"

Perce gritted her teeth. If Eddie had a train of thought, it wasn't an express. She was barely listening as he went rabbiting on about how he'd been in the yard that morning and Mr Latimer had forgotten his briefcase as usual, and he'd come back to his car only someone had parked right up close to it and when he'd tried to squeeze through he'd knocked his door mirror . . .

Perce groaned. "Get to the point!"

"That is the point. That's when I noticed." Eddie paused for dramatic effect. "The rear-view mirrors on Ms Dusa's car!"

Perce glared at him. "What about them?"

"That's why it's strange. It hasn't got any. Not on the wings, not on the doors, and not inside. No mirrors anywhere. I looked."

There was a bit of a silence. During the moment Perce took to wonder whether she had gone mad, or Eddie had, she heard a faint "sssssss" from round the corner, followed by a rustle.

"Eddie," Perce said slowly. "Remind me never to listen to you again about anything, ever."

"Hang on, though." Andy was interested. "That is strange. And what's more, it's illegal." Perce opened her mouth to argue – and stopped. Andy was a car nut. If he said not having mirrors on a car was against the law, then it probably was.

"She could get stopped by the police for not having mirrors," Andy went on thoughtfully. "There must be a reason."

Perce fumed. Just for a moment, she'd thought Eddie might really have thought of something that would explain who the new teacher was and why she made Perce feel uneasy. Instead, here he was talking gibberish and Andy was joining in! "Perhaps she just doesn't like mirrors!" she said irritably.

"Yes," said Eddie, "but what sort of person doesn't like mirrors?"

"Someone really ugly." Anger made Perce spiteful. She glowered at Eddie. "Like you, for instance."

Eddie ignored the insult. "No," he said, in a blood-curdling whisper, "a vampire."

Perce stared at Eddie. "What?"

"Vampires don't like mirrors, because you can't see them in a mirror, so if you're looking in a mirror with a vampire, and it isn't there, that's how you can tell it's a vampire. Ms Dusa is a vampire and that's why she hasn't got any mirrors on her car."

Perce felt herself going cold. Again, she thought she heard a hissing sound somewhere nearby. She shivered. Then common sense returned, and she was furious with herself for being scared. "Oh, leave it out, Eddie!"

"Well, why not?" Eddie had decided to have a sulk. "There was this film on telly the other night, and there were these vampires, and they . . ."

"Eddie, you're cracked. Get real. There're no such things as vampires, and if there were they certainly wouldn't hang around here. This isn't Transylvania."

Eddie was still sulking. "Well, I bet she is. Anyway." He brightened up. "I'll prove it. I've got an idea."

Perce groaned. "I know your ideas. Whatever it is, Eddie, forget it. You don't want trouble with Dusa, she's spooky. Just leave it."

But Eddie had a gleam in his eye. "I'll prove she's a vampire. Guess what I've got in here?" He patted his top pocket.

Perce sighed. "Your chest?"

"Fluff?" suggested Andy, helpfully.

Without speaking, Eddie beckoned them closer. Turning his back on the yard for secrecy, he half-pulled from his pocket a small ornate mirror.

"It's my grandma's," he told Perce. "Dead old. I can pretend it's something historical I want to know about."

"What are you going to do with it?" asked Andy.

"Show it to Dusa." Eddie tapped the side of his nose. "Then we'll see who's cracked." He swaggered off.

Perce was horrified. "Eddie, you can't . . ."

But this time the hiss she had half-heard before was so sharp that there was no mistaking it, and from the way Andy's head jerked, Perce saw that he had heard it too. The rustle came again, too. Not leaves, Perce thought, too soft for leaves . . .

like a coat . . . or a *cloak?*

Perce exchanged a long look with Andy. Someone was listening, just round the corner, and must have heard every word Eddie had said — all the stuff about mirrors and vampires and everything. Right, she thought. A couple of steps took her to the corner of the building . . .

There was no-one there. Perce sagged with relief. There was nothing.

Perce stopped, and sniffed. Well, not quite nothing. There was an aroma. A strange, heavy sort of perfume that Perce had smelt before. She had smelt it for the first time a few days ago.

The day Ms Dusa had arrived.

That night, her mum wanted to know why Perce was rummaging around in her spice jars.

"Garlic?" spluttered Perce's mum. "What do you want garlic for? You don't like garlic. You can't stand garlic. You say garlic makes you sick. When we went to Majorca, you wouldn't eat anything but steak and chips."

"I don't want to eat it."

"Huh. For school, then, is it?"

"In a way," Perce hedged.

Her mum found her some garlic granules, which was as close as she could get, though Perce wasn't sure they counted. Still, they were the best she could do. Now, what was it they did in Dracula films?

Perce wore her arms out trying to rub garlic granules round her bedroom door and the window. This is silly, she thought, even as she was doing it. It's a total waste of time. She thought about Ms Dusa getting into her room in the middle of the night and rubbed harder.

Before she got into bed, she sprinkled garlic granules on her sheets. Then she lay down, closed her eyes, and wriggled uncomfortably. It was like trying to sleep in a bed full of biscuit crumbs.

It took Perce ages to get to sleep, and when she did, she had a dream.

To begin with, Perce was in a kind of temple with marble columns and statues. She'd heard a sound like gas escaping, and strange rustlings. She had turned and run from column to column, peering in all directions, but no matter how quickly she turned, or how swiftly she ran, the sound always seemed to come from behind her. At length, the sound had stopped. Perce, sagging with relief, had turned away from the shadows – to find herself transfixed as she found herself face to face with Ms Dusa.

Looming balefully over Perce, and with a smile of dreadful triumph on her face, Ms Dusa had reached up and slowly taken off her sun glasses. Her eyes glowed a fiery red: but as Perce stared into them, unable to look away, the eyes became deep, deep holes, deeper than the deepest well, blacker than a starless night. Perce's whole body froze and stiffened as she was gripped by the terrible emptiness of Ms Dusa's gaze. She felt herself being sucked into the darkness and the only sound she could hear was Ms Dusa's mocking laughter becoming fainter and fainter . . .

She tried to tell Andy about it on the way to school next day, but Andy wasn't impressed. It was just a dream. Perce couldn't make him understand that this dream had been in 3D IMAX, THX digital and Dolby Stereo Surround Sound. It had also been very, very horrible.

"You're not listening to me!" she accused.

Andy was sniffing the air. "What's that smell?"

"Er . . ." Perce thought quickly. "We had paella last night."

"What sort of pie?"

"It's not any sort of pie, it's Spanish, you dipstick."

"Yeah? What d'you do with it? Rub it on your chest?"

"You eat it!"

Andy sniffed. "It smells as if you've had a bath in it. No wonder you were having weird dreams."

"It wasn't just weird," Perce insisted, "I reckon it was a warning."

"You're as daft as Eddie and his vampires," Andy told her. "You'd better tell him about it."

But Eddie Johnson was away from school. At registration Mr Latimer called out his name and there was an unusual silence. Perce and Andy exchanged worried glances.

"Do you suppose he did it?" she whispered to Andy.

"Showed the mirror to Dusa?"

"Yeah."

Mr Latimer heard the whispering and looked up. "Could I have some quiet, please, whilst I'm taking the register?"

"Sorry," apologized Perce before ignoring the request and carrying on the conversation. "We've got to find out why Eddie's away. We'll go round to his house after school."

Unfortunately, when Perce got home, her mum

went ballistic about the state of her room. "What on Earth were you up to last night?" she raged. "There are garlic granules all over your bed!"

Perce was forced to do a major tidy before grudgingly being allowed out. She pelted round to Andy's only to find that he had been sentenced to a couple of hours' listening to his gran, who had 'just popped round'.

It was nearly seven o'clock, and dark, when Perce and Andy arrived at Eddie's front door and rang the bell.

Eddie's mother answered the door. "Yes?"

"Er, hello Mrs Johnson. I'm Perce, remember me?"

"Perce . . . oh . . . yes . . . I remember . . . Perce." Mrs Johnson nodded vaguely.

"We . . . er . . . we were just wondering if Eddie was alright."

Mrs Johnson frowned as if trying to remember something. "Sorry?"

Perce glanced at Andy. "Eddie." No response. "Your son."

"Oh, Eddie – well, yes, I suppose so . . . why shouldn't he be?"

"Its just that he wasn't at school today. Is he ill?" enquired Perce. She had a feeling that there was something very wrong. She looked hard at Mrs Johnson. She'd seen a similar look somewhere before.

"No, he's not ill. I think he's outside in the garden. Playing. Yes . . ."

Andy looked at the sky in puzzlement. "Playing? In the dark?"

Perce tried to think of something sensible to ask next, while Eddie's mother continued to smile vaguely. After a few moments Mrs Johnson said, "Well, goodnight," and shut the door on them.

Perce stared at the closed door. "What was up with her?"

Andy shrugged.

"She had the same look as the first years did," said Perce. "Glazed and weird." She turned to Andy – and realized that he had already set off down the road. "Hey! Where are you going?"

"Home. Eddie's OK, isn't he?"

"I don't know. Something's wrong." Perce made for the side gate of Eddie's house. Andy, with a sigh, followed.

Eddie's back garden was quiet and full of shadows. There was hardly any light, and very little sound apart from the faint hum of distant traffic. Hanging in the air was a strange, heavy scent that Perce instantly recognised. She felt her mouth go dry.

Straining their eyes, and peering into the gloom, she and Andy could just make out a hunched shape in the middle of the lawn.

"Eddie?" whispered Perce.

"Is that Eddie? What's that he's holding? An umbrella?"

"It's the wrong way up, if it is. Got a torch?"

"I've got some matches." Andy fumbled in his pockets as Perce cautiously approached the shape on the grass. Andy's pockets were always full of

48

various bits and pieces. "You never know what you might need," he kept telling Perce.

Andy struck the first match. "It's a dustbin lid. Upside down."

"What's he holding a dustbin lid over his head for? Eddie?"

"Perhaps he thinks he's a bird table." Andy held the sputtering flame closer to Eddie's face. He gasped, and dropped the match.

Hardly breathing, Perce reached out to touch the motionless shape.

Andy, his voice high and strained, asked, "Why isn't he moving?"

"Get a grip, Andy," said Perce in a strained whisper. "Don't be scared."

"Scared?" squeaked Andy. "I'm not scared. I'm petrified!"

"That makes two of you." Taking the box from Andy's numbed fingers, Perce struck a match. In the flare, they could see Eddie quite clearly. He crouched on the grass; still, silent . . .

. . . and solid stone from head to foot.

Chapter Four

WELL'ARD BECOMES
WELL HARD

"I tell you he was!" Andy bounced up and down in frustration. "We both saw him, didn't we, Perce?"

Andy was surrounded by most of the class. Some looked puzzled, others were sneering. Andy had just finished telling them how he and Perce had found Eddie the previous night, and clearly none of them believed a word of it.

"Settle down!" The class scurried for their seats. Mr Latimer's sudden arrival for registration had made them all jump. Glaring, he fished the register out of his briefcase and started calling out names.

"Lee Adams."

"Here, sir."

"Donna Clarke."

"Here, Mr Latimer . . ."

"They don't believe us!" Andy complained bitterly to Perce under the cover of emptying his schoolbag.

Perce sniffed. "Well, what did you expect? I tried to tell my mum and dad about it last night, and they didn't believe it. Even I don't believe it, and I was there."

"We've got to tell Latimer."

"If no-one else believes us, why should he?"

"But it's true. Eddie was right, Dusa IS a vampire."

Perce snorted. "Vampires don't turn people into stone: they bite them and suck their blood and then . . ." She stopped, annoyed with herself. "Anyway, there's no such thing as vampires. They only exist in books and films."

"Yeah, well, when Latimer calls out Eddie's name we'll tell him what we saw and then . . ."

Andy paused as Mr Latimer suddenly roared, "What on earth do you think you're playing at?"

Everyone turned in their seats to see what had caused Mr Latimer's rage. Well'ard Wally, who had turned up at school for once, had been listening to Andy's story. To show his opinion of Andy's state of mind, Well'ard had turned his jacket inside out and put it back on back to front. He was now proceeding to stick his tongue in his cheek, cross his eyes and scratch the top of his head. His cronies were in fits of giggles. Well'ard was lisping, in his best Quasimodo voice: "Turned to thtone, he was, like a gargoyle, it wath *thyocking!*"

Most people Mr Latimer yelled at had the sense

to cower down behind their tables and keep quiet, but sense had never been one of Well'ard's strong points. "I'm just bein' Andy, sir," he yelled cheerfully, "he's gone mental."

Mr Latimer took a deep breath. "I'll talk to you later, Walter. Michael Gittens . . ."

"Here, sir."

Andy dug Perce in the ribs. "He's going to call Eddie's name – tell him!" Perce felt her mouth go dry.

"Raymond Howells."

"Here, sir."

"Edward Johnson."

"Sir!" Perce's hand shot up. Mr Latimer stared at her. "About Eddie, sir, he's . . ."

The classroom door opened and Ms Dusa wafted into the room. She sailed across the floor to Mr Latimer's desk, and stood waiting. Perce sank down into her chair and forgot to breathe

"Mr Latimer." Ms Dusa's voice was brisk and businesslike. Perce realised with a shock she had never heard her speak before – at least, never while she had been in the same room.

Mr Latimer scowled at Ms Dusa but said nothing. With a frosty little smile, she continued, "I took a telephone message earlier. From Mrs Johnson. Apparently Eddie isn't at all well and may be away from school for some time."

Perce and Andy exchanged horrified glances. Dusa had managed to get in first with the news.

"He'll never believe us now," moaned Andy. Perce nodded grimly. If they said, 'Sir, something's happened to Eddie,' he'd just say, 'Yes, thank you, Priscilla, I am aware of that.' They were sunk.

"Eddie was feelin' a bit stiff this mornin', sir," Wellard chimed in.

"Walter!" Mr Latimer's voice had knives in it.

"But he was, sir – Andy said."

"That will do!"

Perce looked up to see Mr Latimer staring at Ms Dusa. It was obvious that he thought very little of her. Nevertheless, he replied politely enough, "Thank you, Ms Dusa."

"Not at all." Ms Dusa scanned the class. Her gaze rested on Perce. She smiled before turning back to Mr Latimer. "I have to get some art materials from the store. I wonder if one of your pupils could help me . . . perhaps – Priscilla?"

How does she know my name? thought Perce in a panic. Andy looked at her open-mouthed. Perce's body seemed suddenly out of her control as she lurched clumsily to her feet.

"Yes, yes, by all means." Mr Latimer waved an irritable hand. Perce followed Ms Dusa in a daze; as she left the room she heard him snarl, "As for you, Walter . . ." Then the door closed.

Inside the art stockroom, Ms Dusa closed the door softly and turned with a smile as cold as the north wind. Perce could smell her perfume; she had last smelt it, barely lingering, as she had knelt in Eddie's garden. Anger boiled in her. She forgot how you were supposed to talk to teachers. Fists clenching involuntarily, she faced Ms Dusa. "What did you do to Eddie?"

Ms Dusa didn't, as Perce had half expected, raise her voice in indignant denial or tell Perce not to speak to her like that. She merely allowed a brief, wintry smile to play around her lips. "Poor Eddie," she purred. "How dangerous curiosity can be."

Perce tensed, ready in her fury to hurl herself

at that taunting smile, but Ms Dusa laughed softly and Perce felt her will to move drain away.

"Priscilla." Perce nodded dumbly. "I expect your
friends call you . . . Perce?"

There was a hissing noise. Perce recognised it as
the sound she had heard in the playground when
Eddie . . . Perce gulped . . . when Eddie had told
them about the mirrors.

"I've been looking for you for a long time . . .
Perce." Ms Dusa's eyes seemed to glow: the opaque
dark glasses shone red around the edge as though

tiny fires burned underneath them. "A very long
time."

Perce was paralysed. Her brain was shouting
"Run!" but her feet weren't paying attention. The

hissing grew. It was like the sea on a shingle beach mixed with a thousand cat fights. Ms Dusa moved one hand very slowly towards her dark glasses. Perce stared in horror. Were her eyes playing tricks? She could have sworn she saw the turban Ms Dusa wore start to writhe and bulge as if it were alive . . .

Ms Dusa's hand seized the rim of her glasses. Perce braced herself. Some instinct told her that terrible things were about to happen. She tried to shut her eyes and turn away, but couldn't. Her gaze was drawn to the face and the eyes of Ms Dusa. Her dream was becoming real . . .

"Oy, missus!"

Ms Dusa whirled round. Perce gasped as the spell was broken.

Well'ard's head poked round the edge of the door. "Mr Latimer sez I got to help carry stuff." He pushed the door wide open and wiped his nose on his sleeve.

For a moment, Ms Dusa clenched her fists and seemed about to fly at Well'ard. Then a second-year class spilled out of its room, clattering past the open door on its way to the hall. Without a word, Ms Dusa turned to the shelves and started loading Perce and Wellard with paintpots and sugar paper.

The rest of the morning was uneventful. Perce had made her delivery to Ms Dusa's room and escaped. At break, Andy had been desperate for details, but Perce had given him only the barest account. However, as the bell went for lunch and the class stampeded out into the yard, she caught Andy's sleeve and dragged him back into the classroom.

"Come on, Perce," protested Andy, "it's lunch, all the chips will be gone."

"You eat too many chips." Turning, Perce placed herself in front of the door, so that short of walking straight through her, Mr Latimer couldn't get out of the classroom.

Finding his escape blocked, Mr Latimer sighed. "Was there something you wanted, Priscilla?"

"It's about Ms Dusa, sir."

Mr Latimer looked uncomfortable. "I never discuss other teachers with children, Priscilla. You know that."

"All right, then, sir, it's about Eddie Johnson."

"What about him?"

"I think you should see him, sir."

Perce ignored Andy's gasp.

"But he's at home ill. Ms Dusa took a message. You heard her this morning."

"She's ly . . ." Perce stopped herself. It wasn't the done thing to call a teacher a liar even if she was. "She's wrong. Eddie's not ill, not exactly. But there is something wrong with him."

"What?" Mr Latimer was becoming interested.

"You'll know when you see him, sir."

"This is my lunch hour, you know." Andy and Perce held their breath while Mr Latimer considered. Priscilla wasn't the type to make up stories. Andy, yes, most definitely, but not Priscilla. And Ms Dusa? . . . Hmmmm. Something funny about her. Mr Latimer made up his mind.

"Very well. We will pay a visit to Edward's house."

As they walked out of the school together, Andy noticed that Ms Dusa's Car was not in the yard.

Eddie's house was deserted. Perce remembered that his mum and dad both worked.

"We have to go round the back, sir."

Mr Latimer knelt for a long time by the huddled silent figure in the middle of the lawn. He cleared his throat several times without saying anything. Then he said, "It appears to be a sort of bird bath."

"We thought that," said Perce encouragingly. "Because of the dustbin lid."

"It's the nuts and bits of bacon rind hanging all over him," said Andy. "Dead giveaway." Perce kicked him.

"It's a remarkable statue," said Mr Latimer uncertainly. "Very lifelike."

Perce opened her mouth but Andy got in first. "It can't be a statue, sir. Who'd want to make a statue of Eddie?"

"What are you saying?"

Perce and Andy exchanged glances. Perce took the plunge. "We think it IS Eddie, sir."

Mr Latimer raised his eyebrows. Perce gulped and rattled on, "We think Ms Dusa followed him after school and somehow she's turned him into a statue 'cos Eddie thought she was a vampire and he had a mirror and she heard him when he said he was going to show it to her and we don't think she's a vampire but we don't know what she is only when we came round to see Eddie we found him like this and his Mum thinks nothing's wrong . . ." and then ran out of breath.

Mr Latimer said, "I see."

"Oh, but sir, we . . . WHAT?"

"I think," said Mr Latimer, " you may be right." He shook his head. "What you just said doesn't make any kind of sense. On the other hand, it does explain the observable facts. It's the facts that don't make sense, not the explanation . . ." He indicated the stone Eddie. "And there's no point in denying facts when they're staring one in the face."

"Oh." Perce had been prepared for anything except being taken seriously, and didn't really know what to say next.

Andy crouched down and gazed at Eddie. "What I don't get is, why was he holding that dustbin lid up when he got stoned?"

"There's only one explanation that I can think of, and it supports your theory," said Mr Latimer. "He seems to have held the dustbin lid up to pro-

tect himself, as a sort of shield you see – which means that his attacker must have been . . ."

". . . Someone very tall!" exclaimed Perce. "Like Ms Dusa! She stoned him!"

"It was her, sir, wasn't it? Ms Dusa?" Andy sounded miserable and scared.

"We have no proof of that. But something is wrong. Very wrong. I must think about it." With sudden decision, Mr Latimer rose, brushed at the wet patches on his knees, and strode away.

"What should we do, sir?"

Mr Latimer turned and blinked owlishly at Perce. "Do? You mustn't do anything. If what I suspect is correct, what is happening here is unbelievably dangerous. I need to investigate one or two things to be certain. In the meantime, keep your heads down, is my advice."

He stalked out of the gate. Perce and Andy hurried after him.

"Huh," Andy grumbled, "it's all very well to say 'Keep your heads down,' but how do you do it? She nearly got you this morning and . . ." Andy broke off as Perce shoved him violently against the side of the house and flattened herself against the wall beside him. "Hey, what . . ."

Perce clapped a hand over Andy's mouth and jerked her head towards the street. They both watched as Ms Dusa's Car sailed slowly past. Peering round the side of the house, they watched as Mr Latimer turned the corner of the street. Seconds later, the Car followed.

Andy looked at Perce. "Perhaps we should follow them."

Perce looked at Andy. "You reckon?"

They made their way back by a different route.

Charging into the yard, late for afternoon school, Perce collided with Well'ard Wally.

"Oy! Watchit!"

"Sorry."

"It's back." Andy nodded towards the yard, where the Car stood gleaming.

The Car seemed to jog Well'ard's memory. "Oh yeah. She was lookin' for you. Someone said."

"Who?"

"'Er from the car. Miss Dusa."

"She likes to be called Ms," said Perce, playing for time.

"Huh. I don't care what she likes."

"You will, Well'ard," said Perce with feeling, "You will."

"Oh yeah?" Wellard swaggered. "Bit of a monster, is she?"

Andy shuddered. "You don't know the half of it."

"What's she gonna do?" Well'ard grinned nastily. "Make you sit in the Naughty Chair?"

Andy was stung. "Actually, she turns people to stone!" It was almost a boast.

"Belt up, Andy." Perce had had enough of Well'ard's sneers.

"Who's afraid of the big bad teacher, then?" Well'ard waved his arms about, hooting with laughter, unaware that Perce and Andy had suddenly become very still, looking at something behind him. "Issums-wissums scared of the nasty Dusie Dusa? Stupid old bat, with her fancy turbines and daft costume, I ain't scared of HER." He finally noticed their stillness. Arranging a cheeky grin on his face, Well'ard turned round.

Ms Dusa stood directly behind him.

"You interrupted me this morning." Ms Dusa's voice was worryingly mild. "Furthermore, you are without doubt the scruffiest boy I have ever seen. What is your name?"

Well'ard stuck his hands in his pockets and his chin out. "They call me Well'ard Wally, Missus – 'cos I am."

"Very shortly, my lad, you may become harder than you think."

There's that hissing again, thought Perce. She tugged at Well'ard's sleeve in an attempt to get him to shut up.

"Was there something you wanted, Priscilla?" Ms Dusa's voice was razor-sharp.

Perce looked at her feet. Ms Dusa shifted her attention back to Well'ard. "Take your hands out of your pockets, boy. And why have you got your tie around your waist?"

Summoning up all his reserves of impudence, Well'ard said, "Because me belt broke, Missus. What's it to you?"

Ms Dusa reached up for her glasses. Perce stared horrified as the turban began to writhe again.

The hissing filled Perce's ears as she yelled,

"Look out, Andy!" and shut her eyes tight. They both turned away and ran. The air crackled with electricity. Well'ard faced Ms Dusa.

In a small, frightened, amazed voice, he said, "Stone me!"

And she did.

Chapter Five

ROCK AROUND THE CLOCK

From her table, Perce could look through the window at Well'ard's lonely figure looking very small in the empty yard. It never moved. The caretaker's cat rubbed round its legs. A bird perched on it. It rained a bit. Perce felt her eyes getting wet. Poor old Well'ard.

The moment Ms Dusa had turned Well'ard into stone (with a crackly, gritty sort of noise amid the hissing), Perce and Andy had sprinted for the school entrance. She hardly remembered doing this, or bursting into their classroom gibbering with terror to find the place in uproar. Mr Latimer had not come back after lunch.

Eventually, Syreeta (protesting bitterly) had been pushed out into the corridor to go and tell the Head; after some minutes, another harassed teacher had come to split their class up among the others. Perce and Andy held their breath as the list was read out; each in turn breathed a sigh of relief. They were not going to the same class, but neither was going to Ms Dusa's.

Then, just before the end of school, came the bad news. A supply teacher was being brought in the next day, but she would take the first years; Perce's class was going to be taken by Ms Dusa. Even more alarming was that Ms Dusa wanted to see everyone's homework, first thing. Those that hadn't done the work would have to stay behind after school. This made Perce particularly worried. She *never* did her homework. Did Ms Dusa know this? And was she using it as an excuse to get Perce on her own? Perce shuddered. She'd have to get the work done.

At home time, Perce and Andy hung about in the cloakrooms until they had seen the Car glide out of the school gate. The yard was emptying as they went out and stood by their classmate's statue. Somebody had pencilled a moustache on Well-'ard's upper lip. Perce had thought nothing could make Well'ard look uglier than he was. She had

been wrong. She and Andy stared at the stone face in silence.

"What are we going to do?" wailed Andy.

"Shut up, I'm thinking." Perce sat on her school-bag at Well'ard's feet.

"We ought to tell the teachers."

"We told Latimer. Think what happened to him."

"What *has* happened to him?"

"I don't know. I'm trying not to think about it."

"Well, tell your mum and dad then."

"I did; well, I tried. The night we found Eddie." Perce curled her lip. "All they said was it'd be a good thing if someone turned *me* to stone, because then they could put me in the garden with the gnomes and have some peace and quiet."

"Parents!" Andy thought for a bit, then burst out, "But why doesn't anybody see that something's wrong?"

"I reckon she does something to them." Perce considered. "Like the stickies in her class, and Eddie's mum. Some sort of hyp-hyp . . ."

"Hooray?" suggested Andy. "Hip hip hooray?" Perce gave him a look. "Hip joint? Hip-popotamus? Hip hop?"

"Hypnosis, you banana." Perce scowled. "She does something to their minds so they don't remember, or so that things look different to them . . . And tomorrow, it's going to be our turn!"

A short, stout woman came bustling across the yard, out of breath.

"There you are!" She stopped in front of Well'ard, and fetched him a clip across the ear. "Where have you . . . OW! . . . been?"

"Hello, Mrs Well'ar . . . I mean, er . . . Wally's not very well," gabbled Perce.

"He'll be a lot worse by the time I've finished

with him." Well'ard's mum wagged her finger under his nose. "Thank goodness that Ms Dusa dropped by to tell me that you were hanging around here. You're late for the dentist. Why are you standing about here when you know you've got to have a filling?"

"The only fillings he'll need now are concrete ones," muttered Andy. Perce dug him in the ribs with her elbow.

Well'ard's mum hadn't heard. "Honestly, trying to get an answer out of you is like trying to get blood out of a stone! Well, don't just stand there, come on!" She grabbed Well'ard's arm and made to walk off. When Well'ard didn't move, she turned on him in a temper. "What's the matter with you? Don't drag your feet, come on . . . well, if you're too lazy to walk I'll just have to carry you."

To Perce and Andy's amazement, she tried to pick Well'ard up and carry him off.

"Ooh, you weigh a ton," Well'ard's mum moaned. "I think I'll have to put you on a diet; you've been eating too many of my rock cakes. Well, you're not having any more until you've lost

a couple of stone. Now, are you coming?"

Well'ard remained as still as a statue. His mother humphed. "Right, if you're not going to move, then you can stay here!"

And with that, she stomped off through the gate and was gone.

"Incredible," said Andy.

Perce was still gazing open-mouthed after Well'ard's mum. "You see? She didn't notice a thing."

"I reckon you're right about that hyp-py thing," nodded Andy.

Perce bit her lip, remembering next day's ultimatum from Ms Dusa. "Come on. The library in town is open for another hour. I've got about six weeks' homework to catch up on."

Andy dug in his ear with a finger. "Sorry, I must have gone deaf. For a minute I thought you said something about 'library' and 'homework'."

Perce's eyes glittered dangerously. "Well?"

"It's just that you've never done your homework before."

"I've never," Perce pointed out, "had a teacher who could turn me into stone before."

"True." Andy grinned. "See you later, then."

"Where d'you think you're going?"

"To play football. I've done all my homework." Perce glared at him. "Oh, Perce!"

"If I'm not enjoying myself," said Perce reasonably, "I don't see why you should either." She turned towards the gate.

"Mind you," Andy muttered under his breath, "some people deserve to be turned into . . ."

"ANDY!"

"Coming." He trudged after her.

But when they got there, the library was closed. Perce rattled the door.

"It's Wednesday," Andy remembered. "They shut early on Wednesdays."

"Why didn't you tell me?"

"I forgot."

"Well, that's me done for." Perce sank down on the step.

"No it isn't. Listen." Andy grabbed her shoulder. "It's swimming first thing tomorrow. If you bring a note saying you've got a cold and can't swim, we can go to the school library straight after assembly. Right?"

"S'pose so." Perce sulked; she liked swimming.

Andy stuck his hands in his pockets and sauntered down the library path. "Fancy a game of football? Let's see who's in the park."

"Might as well."

But the afternoon was raw and threatening rain, and there was nobody in the park. Perce and Andy mooched round by the lake, and, as the light faded, headed for the shuttered café where all the main paths crossed.

In front of the café was the pride and joy of the

Parks and Cemeteries Department, an elaborate floral clock. Not that it kept time of course, it was just a clock face made out of flowers; except that this late in the year it was a clock face made out of withered leaves and freshly turned soil.

All around the floral clock were standard-issue green park benches. Seated on the benches, or standing beside them, were several figures. These were the result of one of the council's bright ideas. They had paid a local sculptor to place lifelike statues of people around the clock. The council had called it art, the local newspaper had called it a waste of the taxpayers' money. Perce called it silly.

"Spooky, aren't they?" Andy sat down beside one of the figures, a woman in a coat and boots.

Perce shuddered. "We'll all be looking like that soon . . ." She broke off, and stared at the seated figure more closely.

"We could always bunk off. Or run away to sea. Like they did in the old days. I could be a cabin boy, and you could be ship's cook. I know your cooking's terrible, you nearly poisoned us all when you made those scones . . ."

Perce was examining the statue of the woman, reaching out, but not touching it. She stared very hard at the face.

". . . but I suppose sailors wouldn't mind that, they eat maggots and weevils and all sorts of . . ." Andy paused as Perce drew her breath in sharply. "What's up with you?"

"That statue you're sitting by." Perce was breathing hard. "Recognise anything familiar about it, or rather, *her?*"

"Familiar? Perce, it's only a mouldy old stat . . . . . . tue." Andy had turned to look at the face. His jaw dropped. "No, it can't be."

"Why not?" Perce asked savagely. "She turns kids into stone, why not grown-ups?"

"Millsey," breathed Andy.

They stared fixedly at the stone figure of their old class teacher, Miss Mills.

"That's how Dusa got the job. She stoned Millsey."

"But why?" Perce was almost frantic. "I keep thinking Ms Dusa came here because of something to do with us, with me, but I've never met her before, I don't know who she is, why does she want *me*?"

"Dunno." Andy looked around at the figures. "I *thought* there were more than there used to be…"

He and Perce looked at each other wildly.

"Do you think . . .?"

"Could she have . . .?"

They pelted round the circle of figures, sagging with relief at each unfamiliar face, until they reached the far side of the circle, and stopped very suddenly.

The figure was holding a book, at arm's length, gripped in front of him like a sort of shield. If that had been the idea, it hadn't worked.

Andy read the title. Greek Myths. He cleared his throat. "Why is he holding a book about Greek myths? Do you think it could be a clue?"

Perce said nothing. Her lip quivered. First Miss Mills. Then Eddie, and Well'ard. And now . . .

She gazed up at Mr Latimer's stone face, and tears rolled down her cheeks.

Chapter Six

MYTH INFORMATION

Perce didn't sleep well that night. The shock of finding Miss Mills and Mr Latimer turned to stone and the questions whizzing around inside her head kept her awake. 'Who? What? How? Why? When?' Perce couldn't even think straight about the questions, let alone the answers. It had been all she could do to forge a convincing note from her parents to get out of swimming (she had ditched Andy's idea of a cold in favour of a stomach-ache – it would be far easier to hold her belly and groan occasionally than it would be to wander around all day going "aaa-choo!")

When her radio alarm blared out the next morning, Perce wondered whether she should go to school at all. She didn't feel in any state to do her homework even if she did succeed in bunking off her swimming lesson, and Dusa was expecting it in today, or else . . .

Perce thought she could try the old trick of putting muesli down the toilet, making retching noises, and claiming to her mum and dad that she had been ill: ". . . and come and look at it if you don't believe me . . ." It had worked before and would probably work again. But then she thought about Eddie – being at home hadn't helped him. She could just imagine the scene: Ms Dusa at her front door: "Just visiting to check that you're all right, Priscilla. Shall we take a stroll in the garden?" And then . . .

Perhaps it would be better to go to school – safety in numbers. Perce dragged herself out of bed.

In the bathroom she stared at her reflection in the mirror. She looked awful – great big bags under her eyes . . . Eyes. Dusa. The questions flooded back. Who, or rather *what*, was Ms Dusa? Why did Perce feel as though she knew her? She ran through the incidents: the Car, the stickies glazed looks, Eddie, mirrors, the hissing, turning people into stone, Millsey, Latimer. And why had Latimer been holding a book on Greek myths? Surely there must be an answer among all those clues?

"Hurry up in there!" Perce jumped as her mum banged on the door. "You'll be late for school."

"That's the idea," muttered Perce as she swilled her face with water.

"It's Jonesy on duty," announced Andy as he and Perce hovered outside the school library. "What should we tell her? The truth?"

"What truth do you mean?" inquired Perce sweetly. "The truth that we've come in late to avoid Ms Dusa and we're skiving off swimming so that I can do my homework and not get turned into stone? Was that the truth you had in mind?"

"Well, when you put it like that . . ."

"Leave this to me." Perce elbowed her way into the library. The doors swung open.

"Ssssshhhhh!" hissed Mrs Jones.

"But we haven't even said anything," protested Andy.

"Well, I'm warning you before you do," answered Mrs Jones. "No noise. Now what do you want?"

"I can't do swimming so Ms Dusa told me to come here and do some work," Perce lied.

"Where's your note?"

Perce smiled and handed over a carefully forged letter. It had taken ages and loads of practice to get her mum's handwriting just right, but it had paid off on several occasions.

"Hmm," muttered Mrs Jones. "And where's yours?" she asked Andy.

Andy gave her his here's-one-I-prepared-earlier excuse. "Ms Dusa forgot to give it me back."

"Hmmm. Well, make sure there's no noise or

else you'll be straight out."

"Flippin' heck. What a dragon," whispered Andy as he and Perce made their way to a table. The only other pupil in the library was a girl, head buried in a book, sitting at a table opposite.

Andy slumped into a chair. "What work have you got to do?

"History."

Andy groaned. "I hate history."

"You'll *be* history if you don't shut up!"

"Shhhh! If you want to work in here, you must be QUIET." Mrs Jones's screech made the windows rattle.

"Sorry." Perce pointed at Andy and rolled her eyes to show that he was the one making the noise. Andy glared at her.

"Get that big book on Vikings for me," hissed Perce as she began taking a pencil and pencil sharpener from out of her bag.

"Get it yourself!"

Perce turned on Andy. "Do you know what horrible things the Vikings did to their enemies?"

"Er, no."

Perce sharpened the pencil with exaggerated

turns. She took it out of the sharpener and looked carefully at the pointy end. "Would you like me to show you?"

"Which book was it you wanted?" Andy replied quickly.

"The one about Vikings."

"Which one is it?"

Perce gritted her teeth. "It's the one that says 'Vikings' in big letters on the cover."

Andy grudgingly went over to the shelf and picked up the book. He threw it on the table.

Mrs Jones glared. "Shhhhhh!"

"Yeah, alright," muttered Andy. He fidgeted for a bit. "Perce, why am I here?"

"Would you rather be with Dusa?" asked Perce.

"Good point. But what can I do?"

"You're in a library, so perhaps you could read a book." Perce could be dead sarcastic when she wanted to be.

"What book?"

Perce got up, picked up the nearest book and slammed it down next to Andy.

"Sshhhhhhhh!"

"Now look what you've done!" snarled Perce.

"We'll get thrown out if you're not careful."

"Me?" protested Andy.

"SSSSSSSSSSHHHHHHHHH!"

Perce and Andy buried their heads in the books.

Andy read the title of his book. *Myths of Ancient Greece*. He grinned. "Hey, Perce do you reckon when a myth gets married it becomes a mythyth?"

Perce clenched her fist and placed it under Andy's nose.

"I'll read this and shut up, honest."

Andy opened the book. Greek myths. Funny – where had he seen a book on Greek myths recently? He began to flick through the pages.

There were pictures of incredible creatures: the Cyclops, a giant who only had one eye; the Minotaur, half-man, half-bull who lived in a maze. The Harpies, evil women with wings, and Cerberus, the three-headed dog who guarded the gates of Hell.

Andy glanced up. "Hey, look at this – a postman's worst nightmare." Perce grunted and went on scribbling. Andy sighed, looked back down at the book, and turned a page.

He suddenly became very still and blinked at

the picture that was staring up at him. He let out an involuntary "Uuuhh!" Perce looked up, as did Mrs Jones.

"Will you sssshhh!"

Perce scowled. "Andy, you'll get us done."

"Yeah, but, look!" He shoved the book of myths under Perce's nose. "It's her!"

Perce glanced at the picture in the book. It showed a woman's head. Instead of hair, a nest of snakes writhed around her brows. And the eyes . . .

There were no whites, and no pupils. The eyes were red, and seemed to glow on the page.

No turban, and no sunglasses, thought Perce. But you can tell who it is.

She read out the caption underneath the picture. "Medusa, the gorgon!"

Strange feelings flooded through her body. "Medusa – Ms Dusa!" A gorgon. This was what she should have known all the time.

She stared hard at Andy. "You realise what this means?"

"Yes. Our teacher is a cheese!"

Perce gawped at Andy. "What?"

"Ms Dusa is really a smelly blue and white cheese!"

It took all Perce's self-control to stop herself smashing Andy on the head with the book. "You dippo! That's gorgonzola! Dusa is a *gorgon*."

"WILL YOU TWO BE QUIET?!" Mrs Jones stomped over and pointed to the girl at the opposite table. "I told this one lots of times to be quiet but she wouldn't. So I had a word with Ms Dusa about her. Since then I haven't heard a sound out of her. So be quiet or I'll send for Ms Dusa again."

Andy stared at the girl opposite. He gulped.

Perce moved across to the girl and tapped her. There was a hollow thudding noise like a hammer hitting rock. Perce grimaced and shot back to her seat.

"It's Germaine from Class Three."

Andy shivered. "I always thought she was a bit dense."

"Perhaps we'd just better read the book."

"Quietly," whispered Andy. Perce nodded, and they read . . .

The Legend of Medusa

Poseidon, the god of the sea, fell in love with a beautiful woman called Medusa. Unfortunately the goddess Athene became jealous of Medusa and turned her into a hideous monster called a gorgon. Medusa's hair was changed into a nest of snakes and she became so ugly that anyone who looked at her was turned to stone.

A wicked king, Polydectes, ordered the hero Perseus to bring him Medusa's head. Perseus was helped by the god Hermes who gave him a pair of winged sandals, a magical sword and the helmet of Hades which would make Perseus invisible.

Perseus hunted down Medusa to her dwelling place on the shores of Oceanus near Tartarus. Wearing the helmet of invisibility and looking at Medusa's reflection in his shield, he avoided being turned to stone. He chopped off Medusa's head and put it into a bag.

On his way back to Polydectes, Perseus flew over Ethiopia where he found the princess Andromeda, chained to a rock, being attacked by a sea monster. He killed the monster, married Andromeda and flew back to Polydectes who was turned to stone when Perseus showed him the head of Medusa.

"Wow!" exclaimed Andy when he'd finished reading.

"Shhhh!" Mrs Jones hissed.

"Sorry." Andy dropped his voice. "That's her, Dusa! It all fits."

"That's why she wears sunglasses, or she'd be turning everybody to stone all the time."

"And the turban is to hide the snakes!"

There was a gust of air as the library door opened and shut.

"But it says she's dead," protested Andy. "Her head was chopped off and anyway it's not really true – it's just a myth, a story, make-believe."

"But don't you see?" Perce was bouncing in her chair with excitement. "That book Latimer was holding – Greek Myths, it *was* a clue . . ."

"Sssssss!" Mrs Jones's hiss was getting more vicious with practice.

"How can she hear us from over there?" wondered Andy. "Jonesy must have ears like an elephant."

"Sssssssss!"

"Sorry, we will be quiet, honest," said Perce without looking up. "Anyway," she whispered, "its not ears we've got to worry about, it's eyes."

"Why?"

"That's how the gorgon turns people into stone. By looking at them. It's what happened to Eddie and Well'ard and Millsey and Latimer and . . ."

"Ssssssssss!"

This time it was too much for Perce. "Oh sssssh-hhh yourself," she snapped. "Its not as if we were . . . we . . . wwwwww . . ." She tailed off as Mrs Jones crossed the room in *front* of Perce and Andy and went out of the library door. The ssssssssing noise had come from *behind* them.

Andy gulped: "Are you thinking what I'm thinking?"

Perce stared out front, hardly daring to breathe. "You're thinking: 'If Mrs Jones has just left the library, the person standing behind us is . . .'"

"Hello, children!" Both Andy and Perce jumped upright in their seats and screamed as Ms Dusa grabbed their shoulders and peered at the book. "Hmmm. Not a very flattering picture."

Andy and Perce sat quaking, waiting for the worst. It didn't come.

"You really shouldn't jump to conclusions, you know." Ms Dusa's voice had changed. Instead of the harsh rasp that Perce had heard earlier, it was now sickly sweet.

"I mean to say, do I look the sort of person who would turn people into stone?" Ms Dusa laughed to reinforce the point.

Andy started to turn to see if she *was* that sort of person.

"DON'T!" yelled Perce as she spun Andy back round. "Don't look at her!"

"Sssssssssssss!" The hand clutching Perce's shoulder shook with anger.

Perce looked straight ahead and summoned up what courage she had left. "We're not afraid of you!" she exclaimed.

"I am!" disagreed Andy. Perce jabbed him with the pencil. "Ow!"

"I bet it's all a trick!"

"It's a good trick, though. Very good," said Andy, looking at the petrified figure of the girl opposite.

"But it's still a trick," Perce continued, desperate to try and keep Ms Dusa talking and avoid what had happened to the others. "It's probably all done with mirrors!"

"SSSSSSSSSS!" The snakes around Ms Dusa's head hissed furiously. The hand on Perce's shoulder clutched tighter as Ms Dusa winced. "Don't mention mirrors. Nasssty things you can see yourself in. Gorgons don't like mirrors. That interfering brat Eddie realised that. To his cossst."

"SSSSSSSSSSS!"

Andy, realising that Perce wanted to keep Dusa talking, began to join in. "Alright, keep your hair on."

"SSSSSSSSSS!" The snakes obviously didn't like being referred to as 'hair'.

"Anyway," said Andy. "You *can't* be Medusa. Medusa was killed by Perseus. It says so here."

"Ha!" exclaimed Ms Dusa. "Perseus! That coward!"

"He wasn't a coward," protested Perce, "he was a hero."

"A hero?" Ms Dusa snorted with laughter. "And he killed me, did he? I don't think so! I am very much alive as you can see, if you turn around."

"Don't!" Andy and Perce shouted at each other.

The snakes hissed. They were becoming very impatient.

"So what happened?" asked Perce, still playing for time. She was wondering how quickly they could get to the library door and escape.

"We did a deal. I didn't like the idea of Perseus creeping up on me with all the magical things he had been given by those meddlesome gods. And he didn't like the idea of doing the creeping. He hid in my cave, whilst I made a wax model of my head for him to show people. That way, he could pretend to have killed me and I could be left alone in peace."

"I don't believe you, " said Andy, bravely. "I think you're lying."

"Look me in the face and say that, boy!"

"Don't, Andy!" cried Perce.

"Why ever not, if you don't believe I'm Medusa the gorgon?"

"But that happened thousands of years ago. What have you been doing ever since?"

If Perce and Andy had turned round at that moment, they would have seen the evil smile slowly growing on Ms Dusa's face. "Haven't you ever noticed how many statues there are in the world? And how incredibly lifelike some of them are?"

"Stone me!" exclaimed Andy at the thought.

"Don't say that!" pleaded Perce. "Just close your eyes and keep them shut." Andy did as he was told. "Now quickly hold my hand." After fumbling for a few seconds, Andy found a hand. And then . . .

"P . . . P . . . P . . . Perce?" stuttered Andy. "You're holding my *left* hand, right?"

"Right."

"So who's holding my *right* hand?"

Perce and Andy opened their eyes and looked at each other. They both looked at Andy's right hand to see it enclosed by a black velvet glove. A feeling of helplessness began to seep through Andy and into Perce. Perce began to feel heavier. Her will to resist seemed to be melting away.

"SSSSSSSSSSS!" As she began to turn towards Ms Dusa, Perce saw to her horror that green snakes now writhed from between the folds of her turban, hissing and quivering with excitement.

"NO!" In a desperate effort to break free of the spell, Perce shut her eyes tightly and tugged at Andy's hand. Ms Dusa's grip was broken. She tried to grab Andy, but lost her balance and slipped to the floor.

"SSSSSSSSSSS!"

"Close your eyes!" yelled Perce. "Run!"

Perce grabbed the book of Greek myths and pulled Andy behind her as she headed towards where she thought the door was. Chairs and tables went flying and crashing to the ground.

"Ow! Ooo! Ow! Ooo!" yelped Andy as his shins hit the metal legs.

"Shut up and keep moving!" Perce could hear Ms Dusa scrambling to get up.

A few more steps to the left and we're there, thought Perce, dare I open my eyes? She heard Ms Dusa cursing *behind* her. "Yes!" Perce opened her left eye and saw the door handle immediately in front of her. "Got it!" She yanked open the door. It connected with Andy's head.

"OWWWWWWWW!"

Andy staggered but Perce had already pulled him through the door.

"Okay, open your eyes and keep running!"

"I can see stars," moaned Andy as he followed Perce.

But there was no need to run. Ms Dusa wasn't following them. The only thing that chased them down the corridor was the sound of the gorgon's mocking laughter and chilling words.

"You can run, but there's no escape for you. No escape at all."

Chapter Seven

HARD LOOK,
MS DUSA

Syreeta looked down her nose at Perce. "Are you seriously trying to tell us that Ms Dusa is a gorgon?" Everyone else snickered.

The class had just returned from swimming when Perce and Andy skidded through the door in a blind panic. They had tried to tell their classmates about Ms Dusa, but by the time they'd finished telling the story in the wrong order, missing bits out and interrupting each other, everyone thought they were mad.

Another explanation occurred to Lee Adams. "Hey, it's not April Fool's day is it?"

"It's not a joke!" Andy hopped from foot to foot in frustration. "Ms Dusa is really Medusa, Queen of the Gorgons!"

Syreeta sniffed. "And you reckon she's got

snakes under her turban?"

"Yes, they're growing out of her head!"

Lee chortled. "Wait until the nit-nurse hears about THIS!"

Perce banged the book of Greek myths down on the nearest table, cutting the laughter short. "Listen, you thickoes, we're not kidding. All the books have got it wrong, Medusa wasn't killed by Perseus, she's still alive . . ."

"Like Elvis."

Perce glared at Lee. "What?"

Lee smirked. "Like Elvis Presley. Some people think he's still alive."

Perce clenched her fists.

"Yeah, that's right." Ray Howells winked at Lee. "If she's like Elvis, perhaps her favourite music is *rock* and roll."

"And her favourite song is *Snake, Rattle and Roll.*" Lee grinned as the laughter grew.

"And her favourite band is the *Rolling Stones*," added someone else.

"I bet her favourite food is *Snake* and Kidney Pudding!"

"And she plays *Snakes* and Ladders."

The whole class howled with laughter. Perce and Andy stared at each other in dismay.

Lee wiped his eyes. "Hey-hey . . ." He waved his hands for silence. The laughter died down. "It could be a bit of a giggle, though. Listen, when Dusa turns up, we'll all shut our eyes, right, and when she asks why, we'll tell her what Perce said."

Perce was horrified. "What are you on about? This isn't a game!"

"Here she comes!" Mike Gittens, who had been keeping watch, scurried to his place. Everyone stood at their tables and closed their eyes. There were muffled sniggers. Perce shrugged helplessly at Andy – a waste of time as he already had his eyes tightly shut. Perce closed her own eyes and waited, half petrified with fear. We've had it, she thought.

There was a tap of heels on the wooden floor. "Sit down, children." Sniggering, the class groped for chairs. There was silence for a moment.

"Why have you got your eyes closed, children?" Ms Dusa's voice was like syrup. "Are you playing a game?"

Perce heard Lee's voice. "It's Perce and Andy, Ms

Dusa, they say you're a gorgon and you can turn people into . . ."

He broke off. There was a noise like someone rubbing sandpaper on a brick.

He looked, thought Perce. Uh-oh. She put her hands over her eyes.

"Lee?" Syreeta's voice. "Are you all . . ."

The noise again. Perce couldn't stand it any longer.

"I told you!" she yelled, "I told you, you didn't believe me, now she's doing it, she'll turn us all to stone . . ."

"Stop it, Priscilla." Ms Dusa's voice was calm and businesslike. "You're being hysterical. Turning people into stone, the idea! Lee has just gone to get a drink of water, and Syreeta's fetching some pencils for me. Now, if you'll all open your eyes, we'll get on with our work . . ."

But by now, the class was wary. They didn't really believe Ms Dusa could turn them into stone; but now they didn't quite believe that she couldn't, either. They'd decided to keep their eyes shut until they were sure.

"Oh, very well." Ms Dusa's voice took on the

jolly tones of a children's TV presenter. "If you want to play games for a while, why not? What shall we play?" A harder edge crept into her voice. "How about Musical Statues?"

If we do, thought Perce, I know who'll end up being the statues. Feet shuffled unhappily.

"No?" Ms Dusa paused. "Oh, I know a good game – I expect you know it, too. It's called 'Simon Says'."

The class breathed more easily; that sounded harmless enough. Startled, Perce thought furiously. Playing games – what was Medusa up to?

"Touch your noses." There was a slight movement, instantly stilled. "Very good. Simon says touch your noses." Perce heard movement all about her.

"Priscilla, and Andrew, you should touch your noses when Simon Says."

Get lost, thought Perce.

"Oh well," sighed Medusa's voice, "if you don't want to join in . . . Stand up. Simon says stand up. Simon says sit down. Put your thumbs in your ears. Simon says put your thumbs in your ears." People started to giggle. "Waggle your fingers.

Simon says waggle your fingers. Open your eyes." With a shock, Perce realised what Medusa was up to. "Simon says open your eyes!"

"NOOOOOOO!" yelled Perce – but too late.

This time the noise was much louder. Then there was complete stillness. Perce squeezed her eyes even tighter shut, gasping with horror. She's stoned them, she thought, the whole class at once!

"Oh dear, don't you want to play any more? What a pity." Medusa's voice was mocking. "Now, who's left? Just Priscilla and Andrew. Well, well, well." The gloating voice came nearer. "And now there really isn't anywhere left for you to run, is there?" The voice halted right beside her chair, and the gloved hand gripped Perce's shoulder. Perce cringed.

"Yes, I've waited thousands of years for this moment. Waited and planned. Removed obstacles . . ."

Perce choked. "Like Miss Mills, you mean!"

Medusa purred, "Among others. All for you two, Andrew and Priscilla. Just to get you here . . ." – the gloved hand tightened its grip – ". . . right where I want you."

"But why us?" Perce was on the verge of tears. It was all so . . . well, monstrously unfair.

"Don't play the innocent with me!" The snakes hissed furiously. "It took centuries for your family to shrink so far, and years and years for me to find you . . ." She laughed horribly. "Did you think I wouldn't come?"

The pressure to open her eyes was almost unbearable. Perce howled, "But what's so special about US?"

The question seemed to bring Medusa up short. "Is it possible?" The voice was softer, and puzzled. "Can it be that you don't KNOW?"

"H-h-h-haven't a clue," stuttered Andy.

This time, Medusa's laugh was almost merry. "How delicious. I honestly believe you have no idea who you really are. Well, then, my chicks, I shall tell you. It will make my revenge even more sweet."

Perce had her eyes clamped so tightly shut, she could see red inside her eyelids. There was a rustle as Medusa made herself comfortable.

"You see, after I'd helped Perseus get rid of Polydectes – that was part of the deal, and anyway, he had the cheek to send Perseus after me in the first place – after that, I was exhausted. I went back to my island and slept. We snake-people" (the snakes hissed approvingly) "sleep a long time, you know. By the time I awoke, the descendants of Perseus and Andromeda had spread far and wide. I consulted an oracle . . ."

"What's a norickle?" interrupted Andy.

"An oracle," corrected Medusa impatiently. "A person who can see into the future."

"Oh. Right."

Perce had taken advantage of the exchange to begin rummaging about in Syreeta's bag, which hung over the chair next to hers. If only she could find something to use as a weapon – a compass, a ruler, anything!

"The oracle told me that one of the descendants of Perseus and Andromeda would destroy me," Medusa continued. "I would have sought out and killed all Perseus' family, but there were too many. For centuries," the voice became savage, "I was forced to hide, in constant fear that I should be destroyed; but gradually, the family of Perseus spread to many foreign lands, and became smaller and smaller. In most countries, it died out altogether. But here, there remained two families, the last remaining descendants of Perseus and Andromeda, each with a single child . . ."

"Perseus and Andromeda . . . Perce and Andy . . ." Light dawned at last. That was why Perce had always felt that she should know Ms Dusa – some kind of family memory, handed down in the genes from generation to generation . . . It must have been quite a memory for it to have lasted for thousands of years! Perce shivered.

"Perce and Andy. Quite so, Priscilla."

Perce's fingers, busy in Syreeta's bag, closed over something round and metallic.

"You mean I'm related to Perce?" Andy considered for a moment. "Yeuch!"

"Only very distantly, but that is unimportant. You are the last creatures on Earth that could possibly harm me . . . and if you never reach marriageable age . . ."

"Come again?"

"She means she wants to get rid of us before either of us gets married and has children," Perce snapped.

"Ah." Andy licked his lips. "Well, you know, I wasn't thinking of getting married anyway, I don't even like girls much . . ." Perce kicked him. "You weren't going to get married either, were you, Perce?"

"No," agreed Perce hurriedly, "in fact, I was thinking of becoming a nun . . ."

Medusa gave a nasty chuckle. "No doubt, but I couldn't possibly risk it, even if I believed you, which of course I don't."

"How do you know we're who you think we are?" Perce's mind was racing. She knew what she had in her hand – a can of hairspray. Syreeta always used it after swimming, she hated her hair looking out of place.

"Because I have the power to make people see only what I want them to see. That power works on everyone – except for the family of Perseus. You two see what is real. And now, I'm afraid I have no more time for silly games . . ."

The gloved hands shifted their grip. Perce and Andy felt the hair at the back of their necks grabbed and twisted, forcing their heads round and making them cry out with pain. Perce couldn't bear it – in a second, she would have to open her eyes . . .

Medusa gave an evil chuckle. "Here's looking at you, kids!"

With a yell, Perce yanked the aerosol out of Syreeta's bag, tore the cap off, pointed it (she hoped) towards Medusa and pressed the spray button.

"SSSSSSSachurg-achurgh-achurgh-achurgh..."

Medusa let go her grip and screamed as the

snakes coughed and sneezed. Perce risked a look.
The gorgon was pawing at her eyes; snakes
writhed and spat between the tattered folds of her
turban; for the moment she was helpless, but she
was still between them and the door.

"Andy! Get the book! Maybe it can tell us how
to beat her!" Perce stalked the spluttering gorgon,
hairspray at the ready.

Andy said, "It says you shouldn't allow her to
look directly into your eyes."

Perce gritted her teeth. "I know that! What
else?"

"It says Perseus had a magic helmet . . ."

"Brilliant! Only I left my magic helmet at home today!" Some of the snakes showed signs of reviving; Perce blasted them with ozone-friendly, maximum-hold, residue-free salon spray for all-day invisible control.

Andy flipped over a page. ". . . er, and he looked at her reflection in a shield . . ."

"Oh no! Guess what, Andy, I've left my shield at home with the helmet. Does it say how we can defeat her?"

"Well, I suppose you've got to do what Perseus should have done, and cut her head off."

Perce fumed. "We can't go cutting teachers' heads off, dodo-brain. We'd be in detention for a million years."

"You want Medusa to stone us?"

"Okay, okay, so what am I supposed to cut her head off with?"

"A sword."

"Hey, guess what else I left at home today?" Perce gave Medusa another blast of hairspray; to her horror, after a few seconds, the spray gave out. She shook the can. It was empty. The way to the door was still blocked.

Perce threw the canister aside and grabbed the book. "Andy, when that spray wears off we are *geology*. We need a weapon – what's in your pockets?"

Andy rummaged. "I've got a pencil sharpener. . ."

"What am I supposed to do, sharpen her to death?"

Andy brightened. "Hey, I've got my sunglasses – my mirror shades. If you put them on, she won't be able to see your eyes, she'll only see . . ."

". . . Her own reflection! That's brilliant!"

Andy looked puzzled. "Is it? Why?"

At that moment, a howl of rage from behind them froze their blood.

"You miserable children!" Medusa was spitting with rage. "I'm through being Ms Nice Guy. Prepare to be stoned!"

In one movement, Perce grabbed the mirror shades from Andy's trembling hand, put them on, and spun round to face Medusa.

The snakes were writhing madly. The gorgon's eyes blazed. Medusa gave a horrid grin of triumph . . .

. . . which turned to a look of shock, then horror . . .

"No! No! Mirrors! Noooaaarrrrgggh . . ."

There was a rumbling, roaring sound like very small continents colliding. The red glow from Medusa's eyes seemed to spread out over her face and head, along the snakes, down her body. Everywhere it passed, Medusa turned grey and became still. One final flash of red, one last echoing howl of rage and unspeakable hate, and there was silence.

Very carefully, Perce took the shades off.

In front of her stood a nightmare statue. Snakes, now frozen in mid-writhe; a face forever carved in an expression of rage and despair. Stone arms raised to curse, stone clothes, stone legs and stone feet.

"Is it safe?" Andy stuck his head out from under a table.

"See for yourself."

Andy looked at Medusa and whistled. He struggled out from his refuge. "What did you *do*?"

Perce tried hard to stop panting. "It was the mirror shades. You said it yourself. She saw her own reflection."

"Stone me!"

"Not this time." Perce felt herself trembling all over. "Stoned her."

Another sound started to make itself heard – a sort of rustling creak.

"Look out!" Andy dived back under his table. "She's coming back to life again!"

Perce started to giggle helplessly. "*She's* not. *They* are."

Lee, Syreeta and the rest of the class started to move. Colour crept back over their clothes and their faces. There was a lot of stretching and rubbing.

Andy stared. "Well, there's something you don't see every day."

"The spell – or whatever it was – must have stopped working when she turned to stone herself."

There was a roar from the yard outside. Perce and Andy darted to the window. Well'ard Wally was racing round, throwing things at pigeons. He looked upset. Mind you, thought Andy, seeing what the pigeons had done to his head – or rather, on his head – you couldn't really blame him.

Perce's giggles turned to screeches of laughter. Andy turned to her in astonishment. "What's up with you?"

"Eddie – Eddie Johnson!" Perce managed to gasp. "What's he going to think when he finds himself standing in the middle of the garden with bits of fat and a bag of nuts hanging off his nose?"

Chapter Eight

A STONY SILENCE

A month later, school life had settled back into its normal boring pattern but Perce didn't mind. She welcomed the day-to-day routine and even started to take an interest in some of the lessons.

Mr Latimer and Miss Mills had returned and quickly settled back into their teaching duties. Nevertheless, the two of them were still jumpy. Perce felt particularly sorry for Miss Mills when Lee or Well'ard hissed at her when her back was turned. They enjoyed seeing Millsey spin round with a look of horror on her face. Even Latimer had stopped going on about how wonderful Greek myths were. And neither of them could stand pigeons.

Perce and Andy were held in great esteem by the rest of their class. Even their teachers seemed to show them a guarded respect. Perhaps this was the reason they were chosen to show Mrs Osbald, the Chair of Governors, around the school on her annual tour of inspection.

For the visit, the school had been specially tidied. Coats of paint on fading woodwork had mysteriously appeared overnight and kids were warned to be on their best behaviour and told not to mention anything about "you-know-what".

Perce and Andy met Mrs Osbald at the school reception and showed her into several classrooms where teachers were teaching interesting and exciting lessons. "The ones they only ever teach when an outside visitor or a school inspector comes in," thought Perce.

"Jolly good," Mrs Osbald shrilled. "Where to next?"

"Our classroom," said Andy.

"Lovely. Lead on."

To get to their classroom, they had to cross the playground.

"That looks very handsome," said Mrs Osbald. "Very nice indeed." She stopped and pointed to the corner of the playground. Where once the old bike shed had stood, there was now a brand new addition to the school.

A rockery.

Andy stared at Perce with a look of concern on his face. Perce returned the grimace.

"How long has that been there?" gushed Mrs

Osbald. "I don't remember seeing it before."

Perce took a deep breath. "Er – about a month," she replied, "it was part of an environmental studies course."

"Yeah, that's right," added Andy, "it was a sort of recycling exercise. Using – er – unwanted material to improve our surroundings."

Mrs Osbald smiled. "Well, it certainly does that, I must say. I'm a very keen gardener myself. I'd like to see what you've got growing here."

She reached the pile of rocks, put on her spectacles and looked carefully at the rockery.

Perce and Andy held their breath.

Mrs Osbald examined the rockery closely, and the more closely she examined it, the stiller she became. She glanced at Perce and Andy, and seemed about to say something but thought better of it. She prodded about again, gave a little gasp, and straightened up. Perce stared into her eyes. They seemed to have a faraway, glazed look. Andy and Perce led Mrs Osbald back towards the school.

"What very strange rocks." Mrs Osbald looked oddly nervous. She glanced over her shoulder and said, too casually, "I wonder if I could get some like that for my garden?"

Perce looked at Andy. "Oh, er . . . I don't think you'll be able to get any. They were from a very special supply. One lot only." Andy grinned.

"What a pity," mused Mrs Osbald as she gave Perce and Andy a quizzical look. "A very odd sort of stone indeed. Such strange shapes. Almost life-like. They look just like hands . . . and feet . . . and snakes . . ."

About the authors

Steve Barlow comes from Crewe and now lives in Derbyshire with his wife and two children. After working as a refuse collector, a laundry van driver and a puppeteer, Steve went into the performing arts, met the other "Steve" and became a writer.

Steve Skidmore was born in Birstall and now lives in Leicester. Steve enjoys writing books and performing with Steve Barlow.

These two are Britain's most popular writing double act for young people, specialising in comedy and adventure. "The Two Steves" also perform regularly in schools and libraries, delighting audiences of all ages.

VLAD THE DRAC RETURNS

by Ann Jungman

£4.99 ISBN 1-903015-34-0

Vlad the Drac, the tiny vegetarian vampire is back. Now that
he is no longer a secret Vlad wants his phone in the paper
every day and to be on T.V. as much as possible. The vampire's
antics to get publicity get him into lots of trouble but when he
goes missing, everyone is very worried.

*"Funny, unpredictable, playful and defiant.
Vlad is always excellent company."*
Nicholas Tucker in *The Rough Guide to Children's Books*

THE DRAGON CHARMER
by Douglas Hill
£4.99 ISBN 1-903015-36-7

Just because her father is a brilliant dragon
charmer doesn't mean that Elynne is any less
frightened of the great beasts than anyone else.
However, when a baby dragon prince is born
and Elynne realises he is in great danger, she
finds depths of courage and determination she
had no idea she possessed.

*"Elynne is not a brave girl but in this literally charming
story, Douglas Hill shows how love can make heroines out
of the mosy unlikely people."*
Mary Hoffman

YOUR GUESS IS AS GOOD AS MINE

by Bernard Ashley

£3.99 ISBN 1-903015-04-9

The rain hit Nicky hard as he came out of school and everyone ran. It was screams and running feet all along the street, expecially when the thunder started. So it seemed too good to be true when he saw his dad's yellow Mini. But it wasn't his dad's car, nor was it his dad driving and Nicky is suddenly plunged into a terrifying adventure and a frantic race against time.

A sympathetic look at "stranger danger".